CROSS BONE ISLAND

For Paul
the nicest pirate we know

Copyright © 2003 Christyan and Diane Fox
All rights reserved
CIP Data is available

Published in the United States 2003 by Handprint Books
413 Sixth Avenue
Brooklyn, New York 11215
www.handprintbooks.com

First American Edition
Simultaneously published in Great Britain by Little Tiger Press
Printed in Singapore
ISBN: 1-929766-76-9
2 4 6 8 10 9 7 5 3 1

Pirate PiggyWiggy

Christyan and Diane Fox

Handprint Books 🖐 Brooklyn, New York

Sometimes when I sail my little boats, I dream of what it might be like to be a swashbuckling pirate!

I would wear
a big black hat,
a patch over my eye
and have a parrot
on my shoulder...

My ship would be the finest that over sailed the seven seas.

Ten paces north...
eight paces south...

Shiver-me-timbers, X marks the spot!